The Little Mouse and the Big Elephant

Written by Narinder Dhami
Illustrated by Amy Schimler

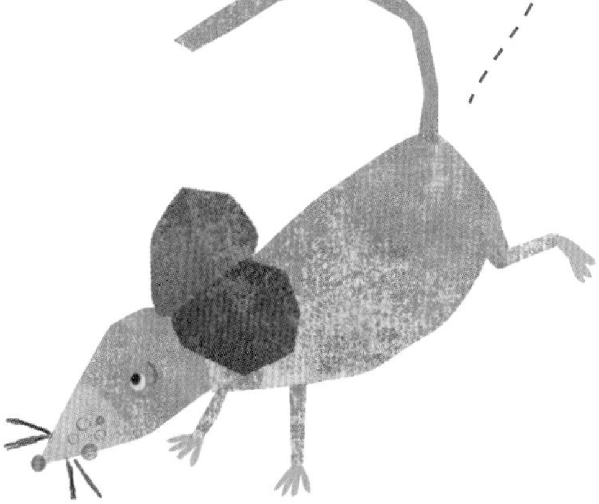

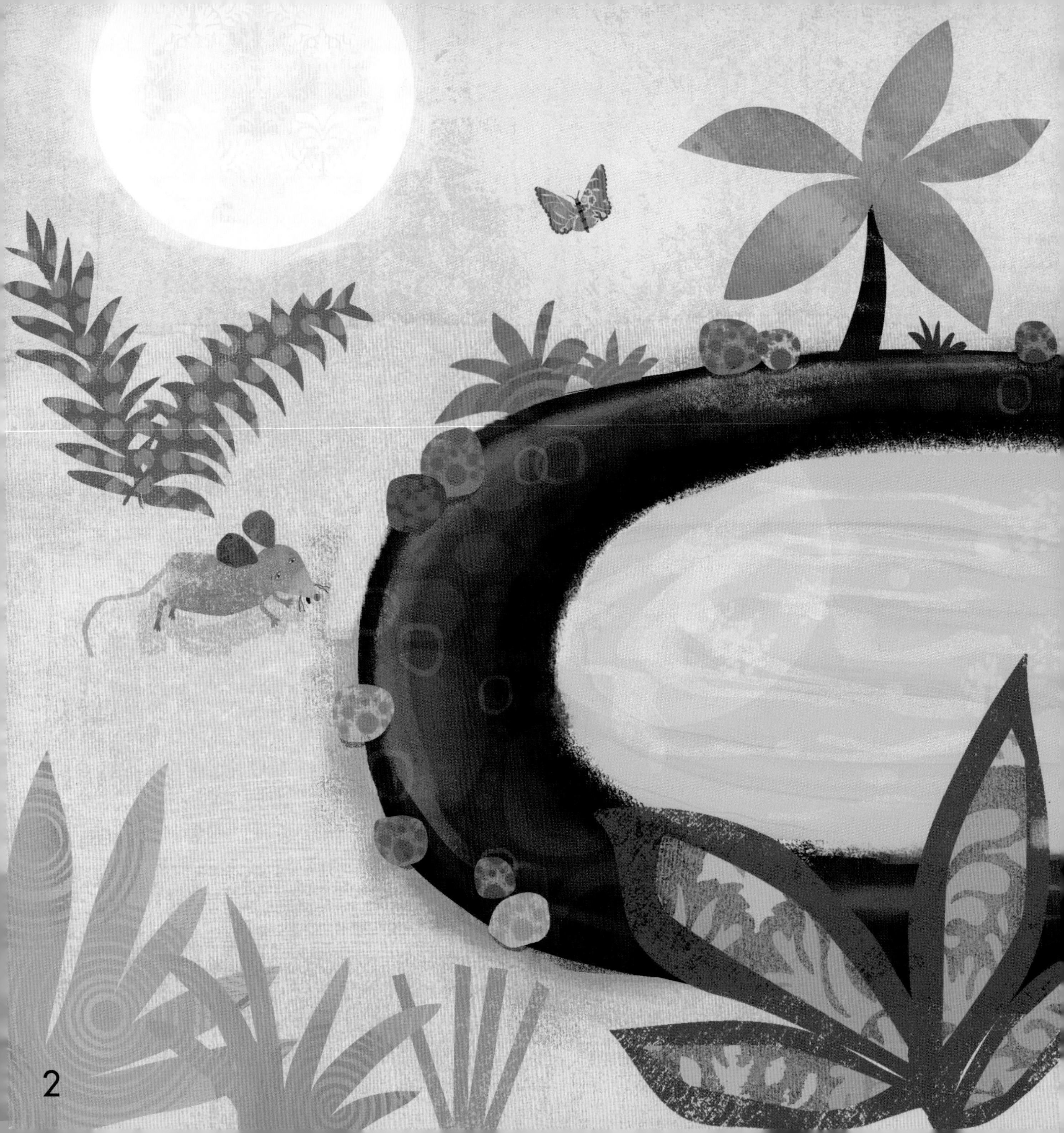

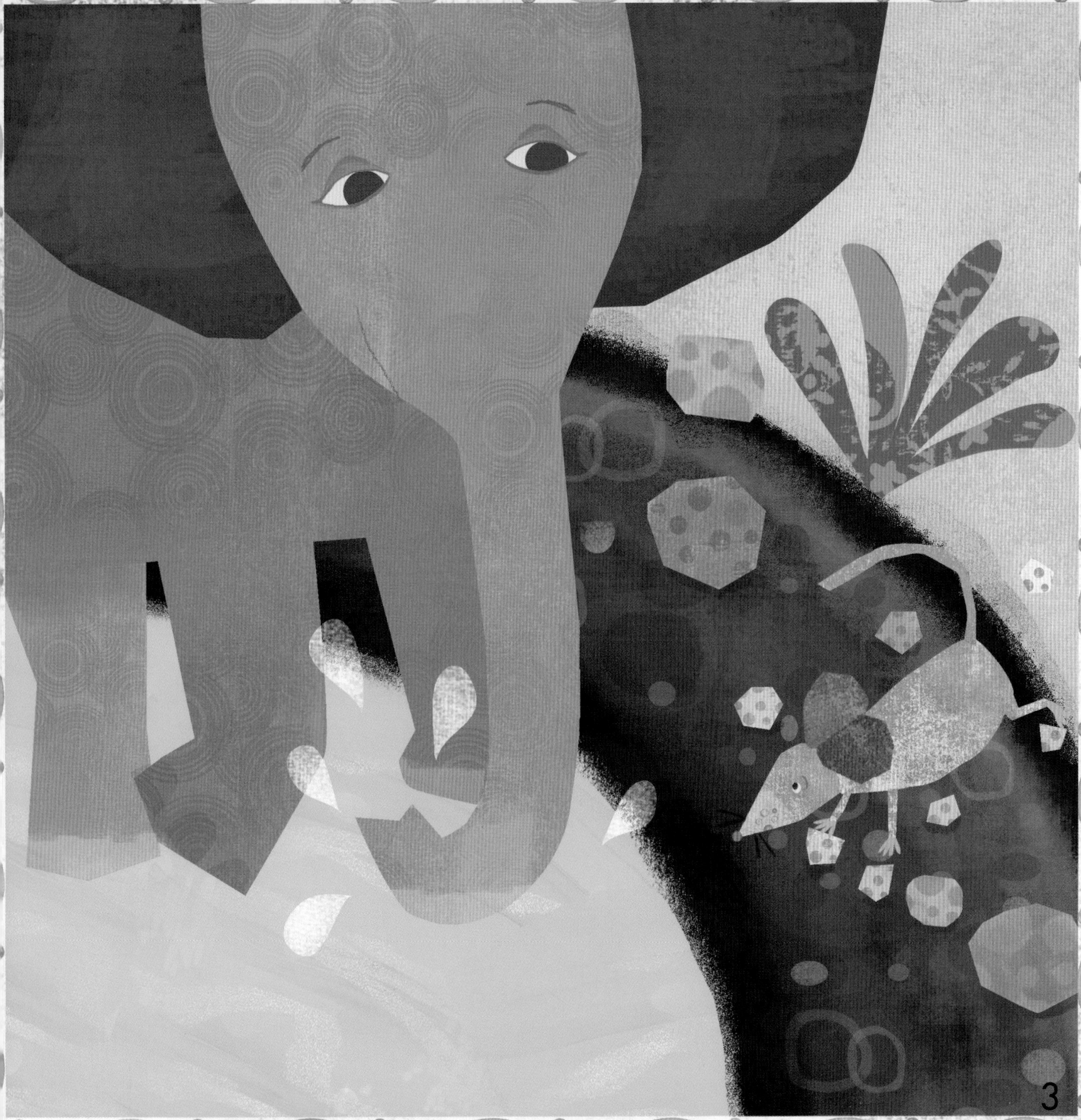

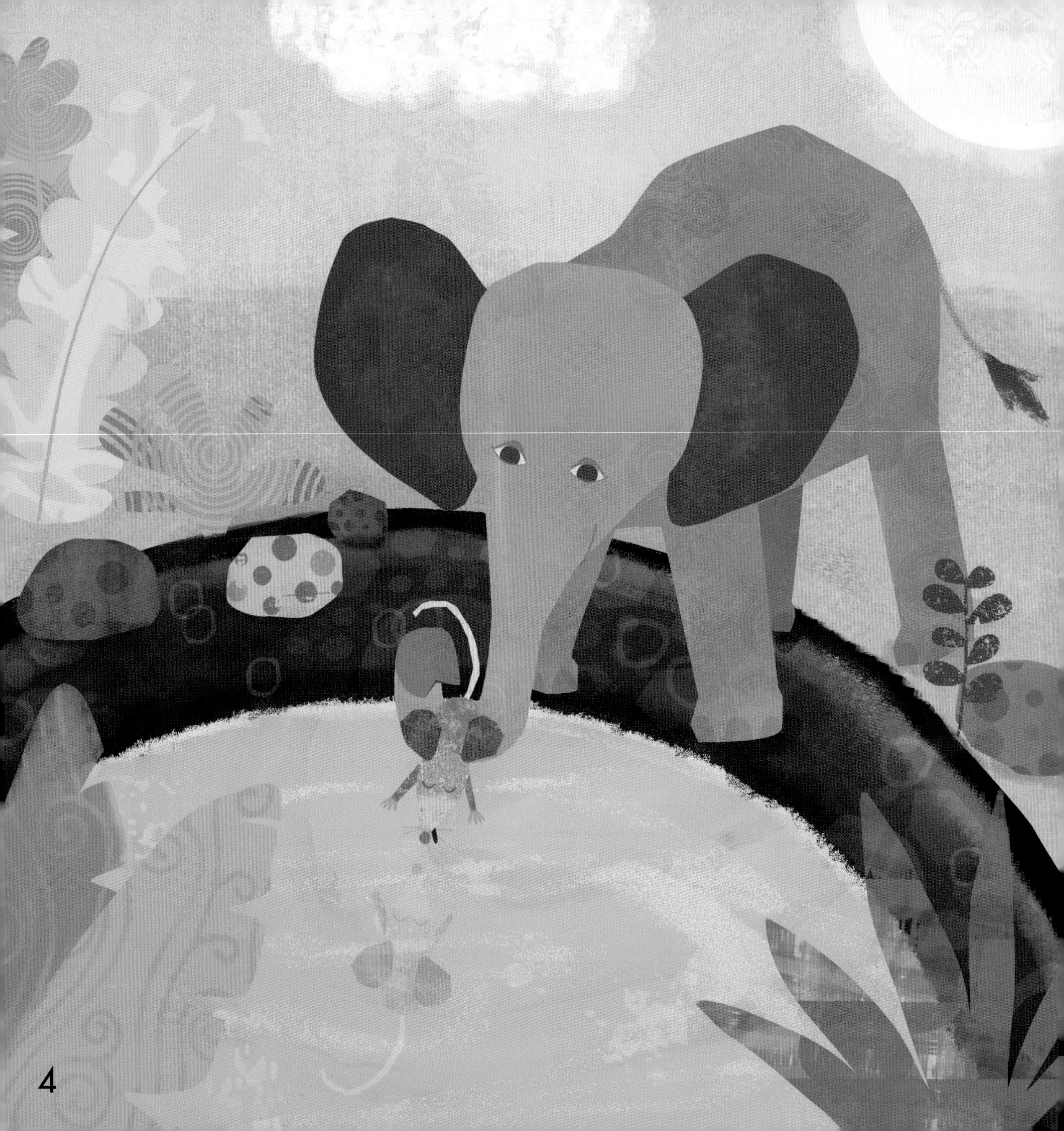

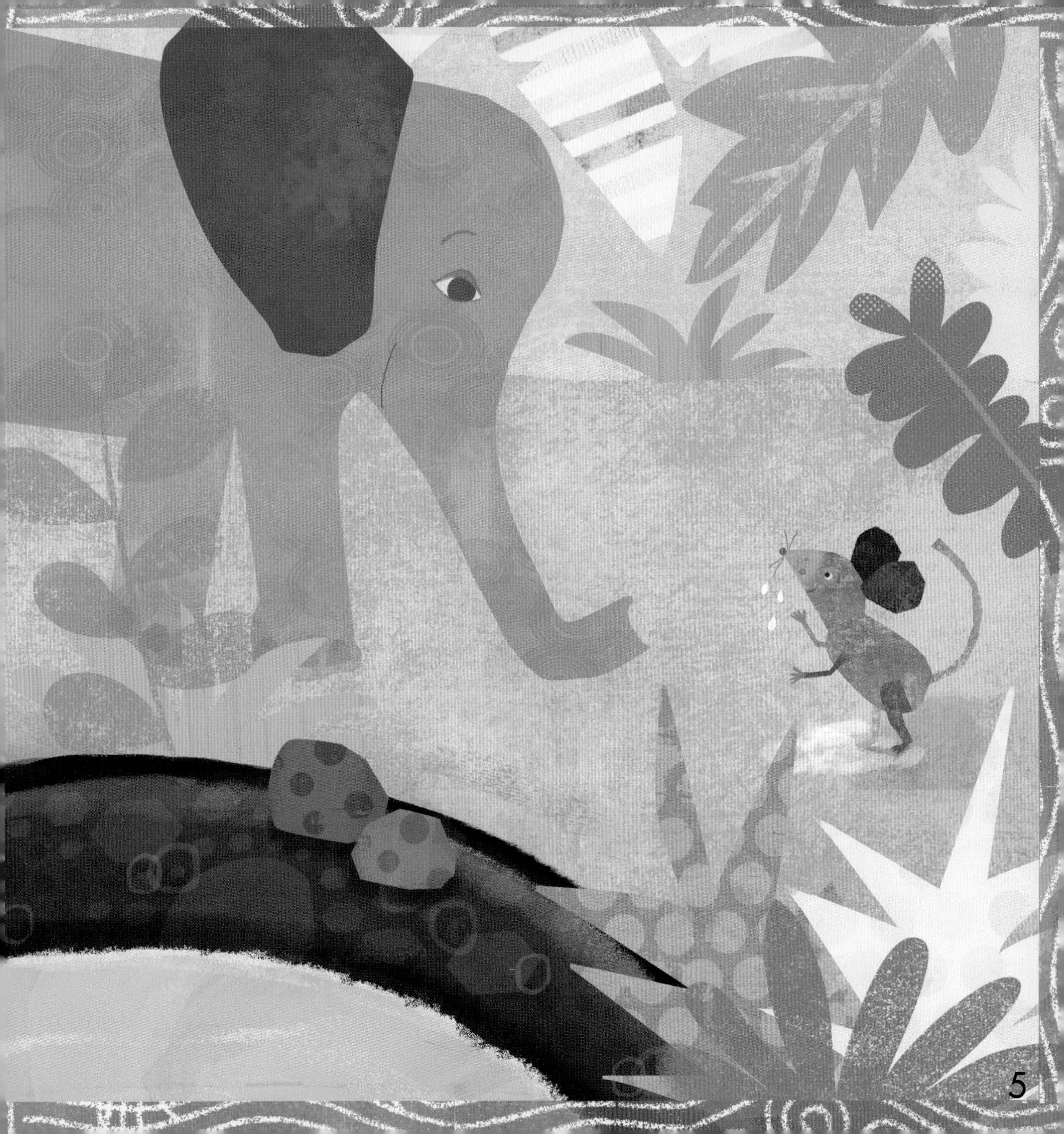

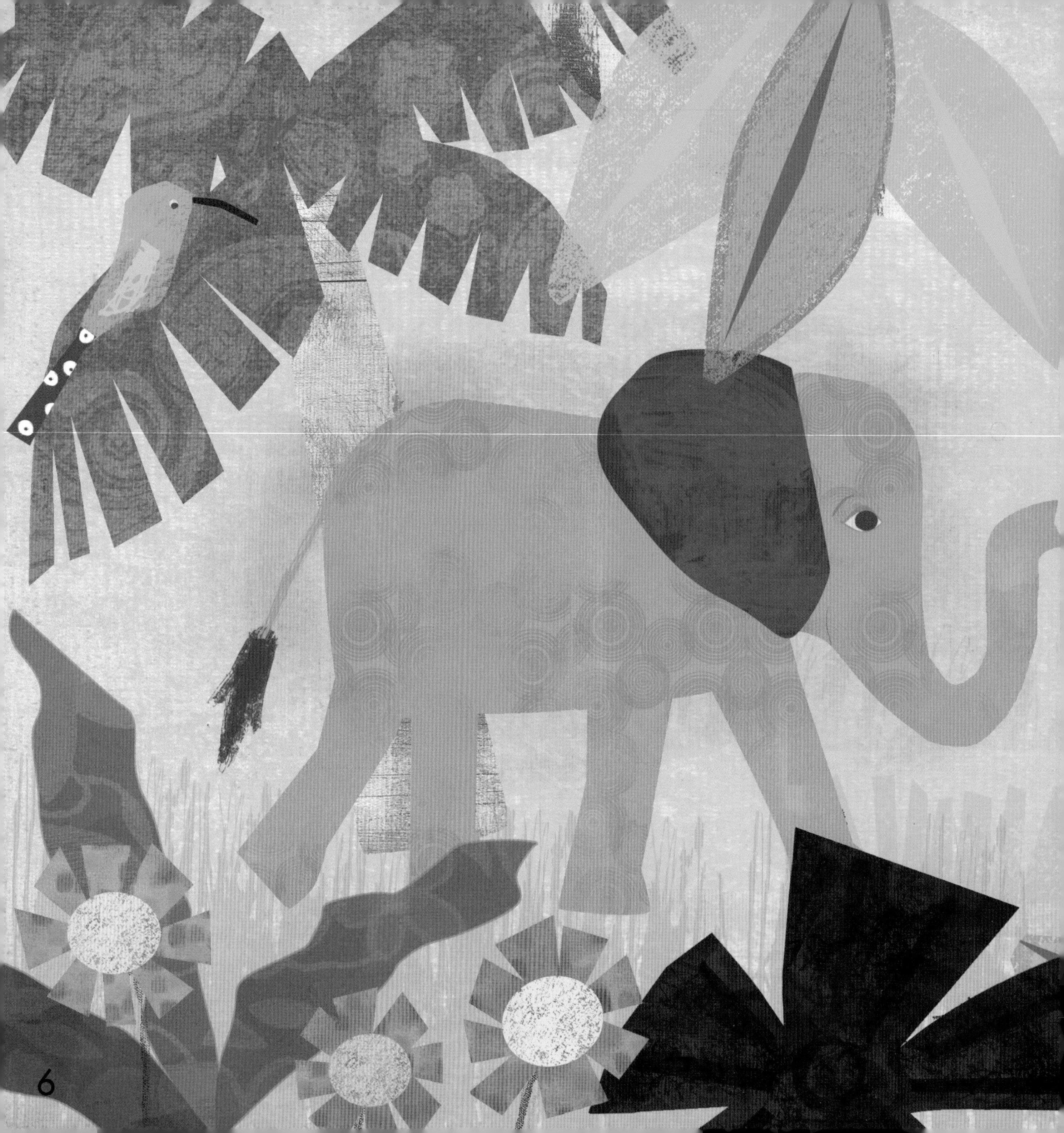

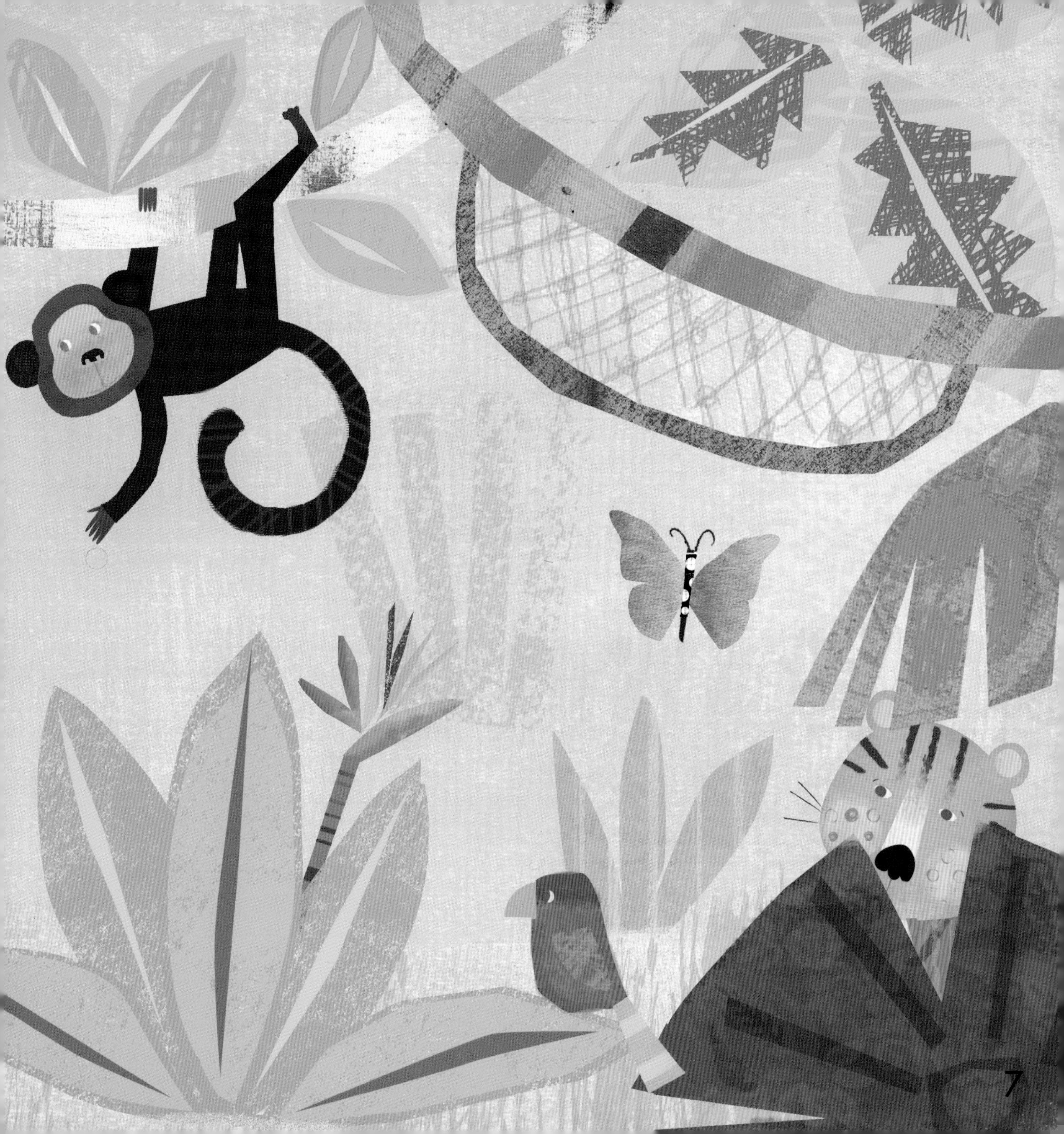

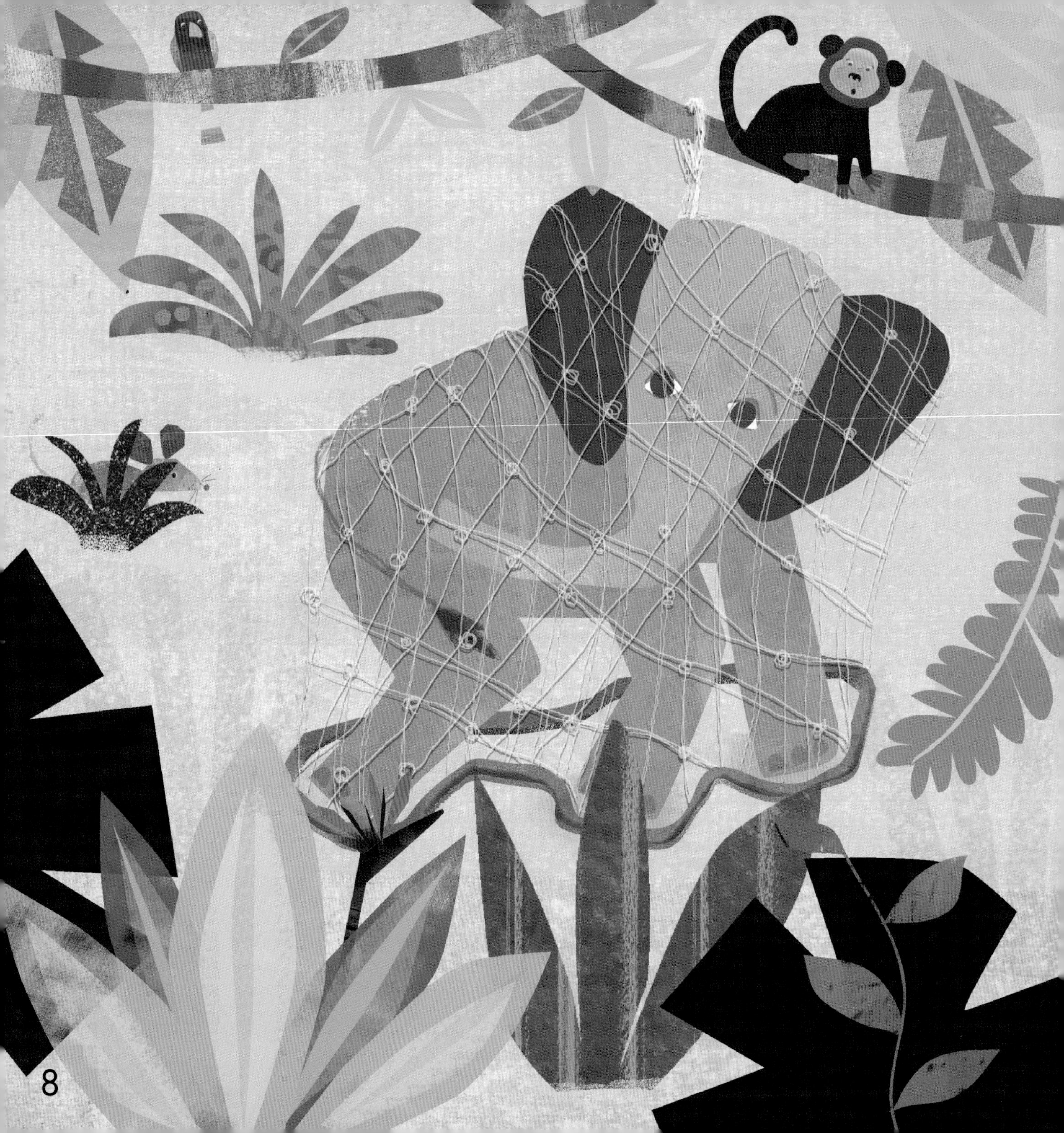

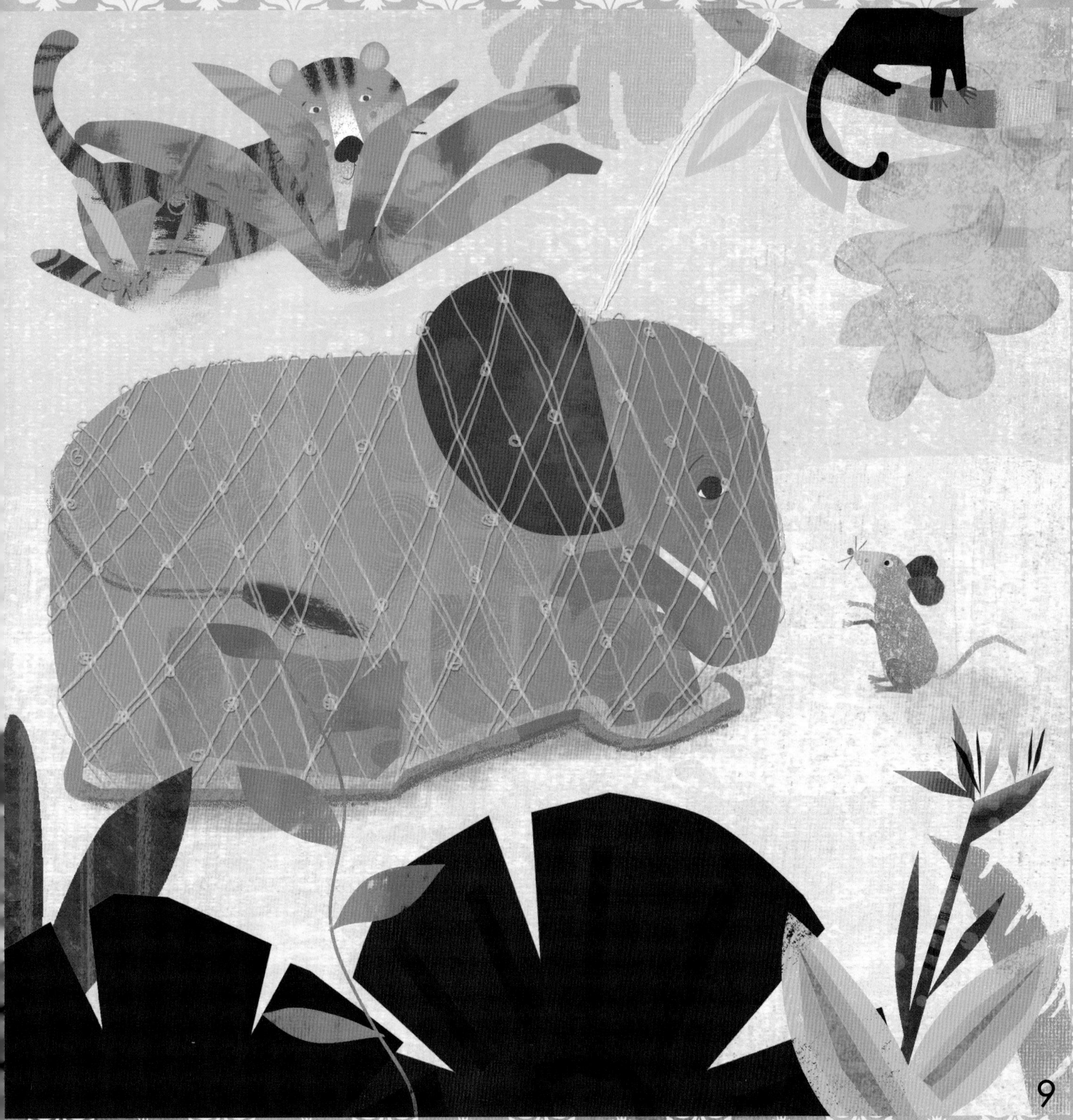

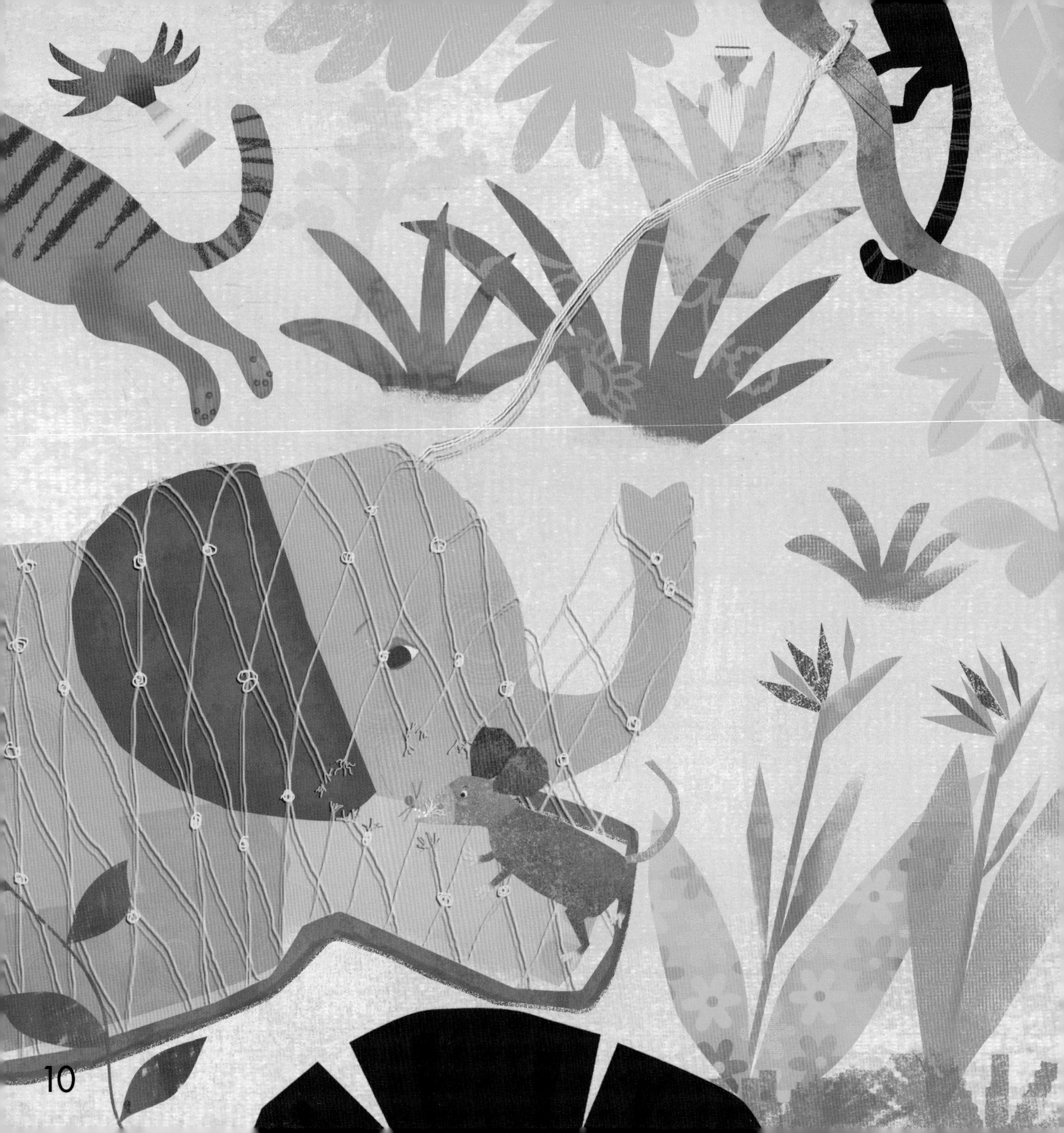

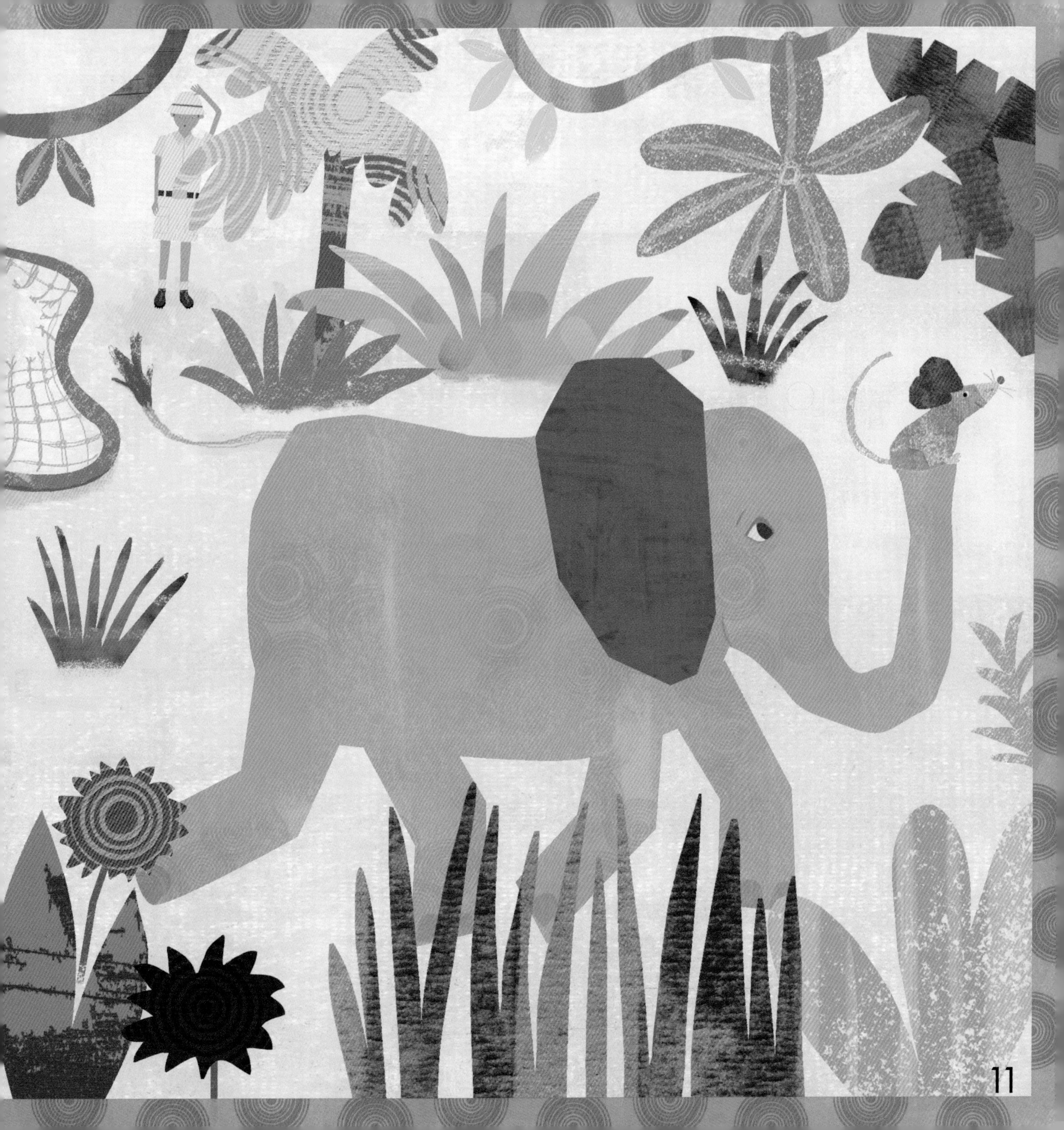

Retell the story

Once upon a time …

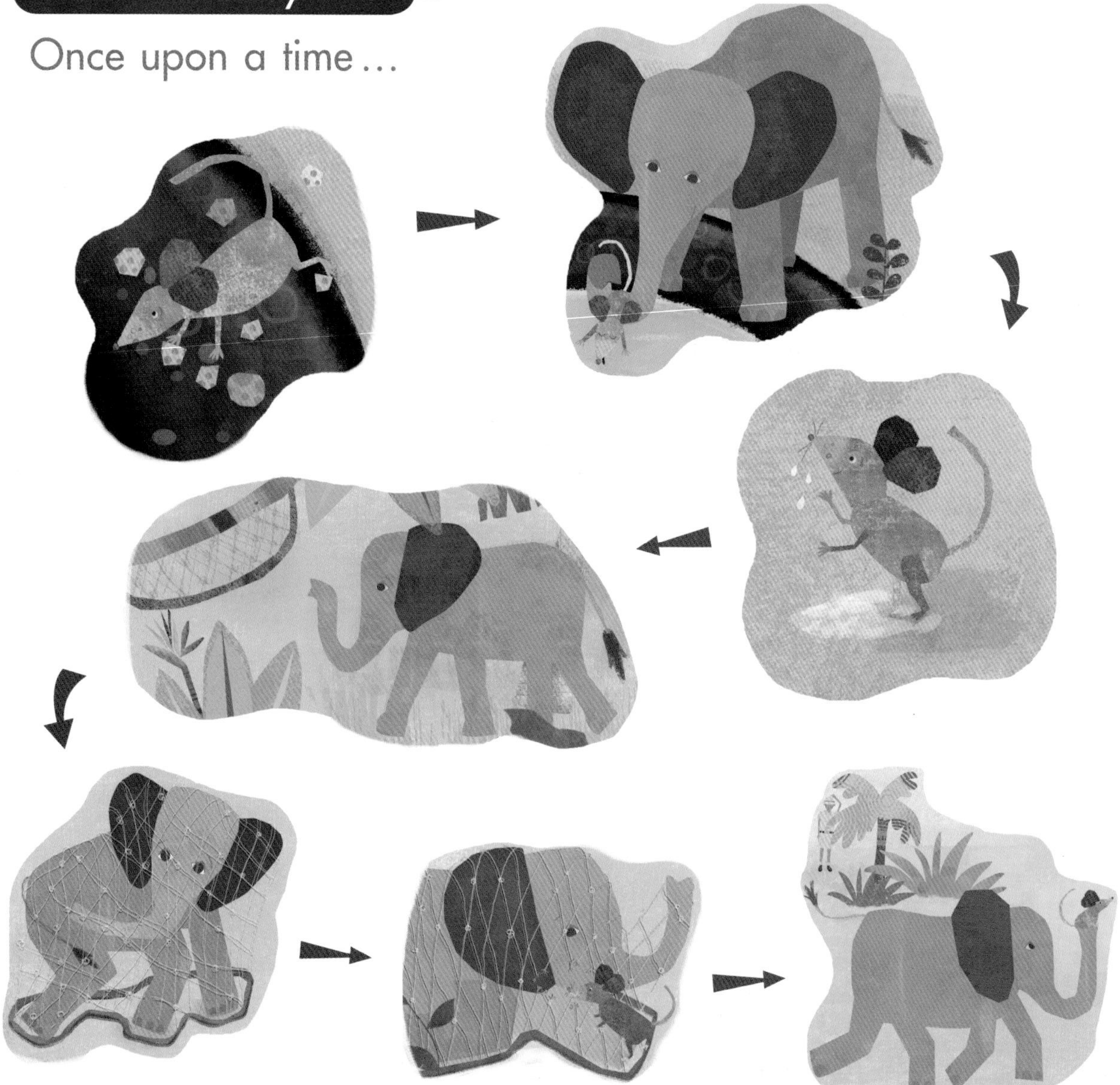

The end.